THIS CANDLEWICK BOOK BELONGS TO:

_____

_____

_____

_____

First U.S. edition 1994
First published in Great Britain in 1987 by Walker Books Ltd., London.

Library of Congress Cataloging-in-Publication Data

West, Colin.
Ten little crocodiles / Colin West.—1st U.S. ed.
"First published in Great Britain in 1987 by Walker Books Ltd., London"—T.p.verso.
Summary: Starting with ten little crocodiles clustered around a table,
the reader counts down from ten to one as a crocodile is taken away in each picture.
ISBN 1-56402-463-6
[1. Stories in rhyme. 2. Crocodiles—Fiction. 3. Counting.]
I. Title. II. Title: 10 little crocodiles.
PZ8.3.W4997Te   1994
[E]—dc20   93-44027

2 4 6 8 10 9 7 5 3 1

Printed in Hong Kong

The pictures in this book were done in watercolor.

Candlewick Press
2067 Massachusetts Avenue
Cambridge, Massachusetts 02140

Ten Little Crocodiles

Colin West

CANDLEWICK PRESS
CAMBRIDGE, MASSACHUSETTS

10

Ten little crocodiles
Sitting down to dine—

One of them ate too much cake,
And then there were . . .

Nine little crocodiles
Trying to lose weight.

One of them tried till he dropped,
And then there were . . .

Eight little crocodiles
Who hoped to go to heaven.

One of them went right away,
And then there were . . .

Seven little crocodiles
Doing magic tricks.

One of them went up in smoke,
And then there were . . .

Six little crocodiles
Learning how to drive.

One of them drove up a tree,
And then there were . . .

5

Five little crocodiles
Sailing to the shore.

One of them fell overboard,
And then there were . . .

Four little crocodiles
Going off to ski.

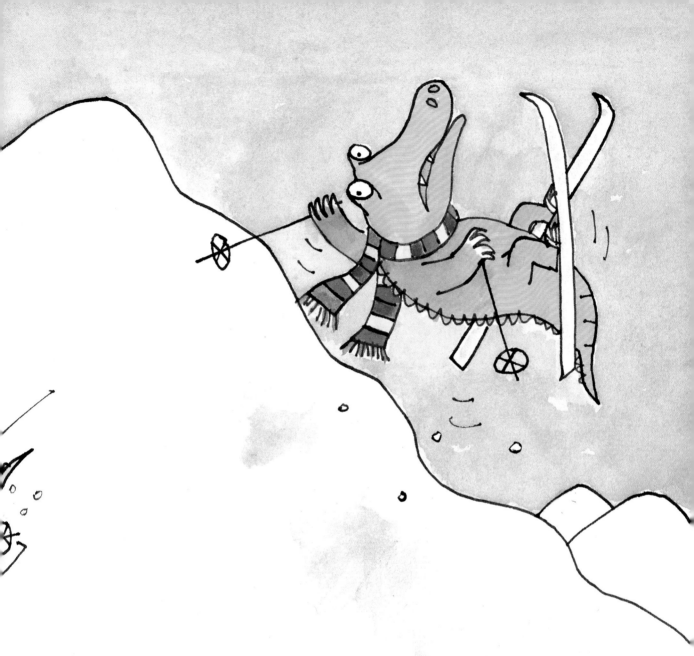

One of them turned somersaults,
And then there were . . .

3

Three little crocodiles
Visiting the zoo.

One of them got left behind,
And then there were . . .

Two little crocodiles
Sitting in the sun.

One of them went home for lunch,
And then there was . . .

One little crocodile
Missing all his friends.

Let's take another look at them
Before the story ends . . .

One little crocodile
Then gets a big surprise—

All his friends are safe and sound!
He can't believe his eyes!

Colin West is the author of many books for children and the illustrator of numerous others. About *Ten Little Crocodiles* he says, "I wanted to make a counting book that was fun, so I wrote with a rhyme that links the verses. I hope children have a good time guessing the rhyme and turning the pages."